HER RISK TO TAKE

A R.I.S.C. VALENTINE'S DAY NOVELLA

ANNA BLAKELY

HER RISK TO TAKE

A R.I.S.C. Valentine's Day Novella

Anna Blakely

ABOUT THE BOOK

Danger found them once before. Now it's back, and this time...the stakes are even higher.

It's Valentine's Day, and restaurant owner Lexi Matthews is finally going to reveal the secret that will fill her husband's heart with joy...and change their lives forever. She's planned the perfect evening, right down to the last detail. But when a group of robbers storm into her place of business, Lexi finds herself trapped in a deadly nightmare.

Two years ago, R.I.S.C. operative Trevor Matthews saved Lexi from a sadistic killer who nearly stole her away from him. Then he married her, vowing to always protect her from that point forward...no matter what.

So when he discovers Lexi, her staff, and a restaurant full of customers are being held hostage, Trevor will stop at nothing to get to her. Because Lexi isn't just his wife. She's the other half of his soul. And if he loses her, it'll be a loss from which he'll never recover.

1

"Hey, angel."

Lexi Matthews swung her gaze from the mirror to find her husband standing in the bathroom doorway. With one of his broad shoulders resting against the doorjamb, Trevor stared back at her as if she were the most beautiful woman in the world.

When she was with him, she felt as if she was.

"You're home!" She dropped the lip gloss down onto the vanity and rushed to him.

Encircling her waist with his strong hands, he smiled wide and lifted her effortlessly. Lexi instinctively wrapped her legs around his hips and locked her hands together behind his neck.

Trevor pressed his lips to hers, and after a thorough kiss full of promises and need, he pulled back just enough to say, "God, I missed you."

"Missed you more." She stole another kiss. "I was worried you wouldn't make it tonight."

"You kidding?" He set her down gently. "No way was I missing Valentine's Day with my beautiful wife."

A familiar heat crawled up her neck and into her cheeks. Though they'd been married nearly two years, Lexi still blushed when he said sweet things like that.

"How did training go?"

"New guys are solid." He referred to R.I.S.C.'s new Charlie team.

R.I.S.C.—which stood for Rescue, Intel, Security, and Capture—was the private black ops company Trevor worked for. It was owned by Jake McQueen, Trevor's former Delta Force brother and best friend, and together, the two men ran the company and led R.I.S.C.'s Alpha Team.

"That's good." She placed a hand on his t-shirt-covered chest. His heart beat strong and steady beneath her palm, the best kind of reminder that he'd once again made it back home, safe and sound. "I bet Jake's excited."

"Guy's like a kid at Christmas." The corners of Trevor's eyes crinkled when he smiled. "Not that he'd ever admit it."

"What about you? How do you feel about the new change?"

"I think the choice to expand to other areas of the country was a good one. The need is definitely there, though it does seem a little strange knowing we'll have three teams instead of just the two. And that the new team will be stationed on the East coast, rather than in Texas like Alpha and Bravo."

"I'm sure it'll take some getting used to, but needing another team means business is good." Lexi glanced at her watch. "Speaking of business, I need to finish getting ready." She went back to the discarded lip gloss. "I still need to stop for gas and make a quick run to the store for a couple of things before I head in."

"You sure you have to go?" Trevor came up behind her. He placed his hands on her hips before slowly running them up her sides, along her ribs. His thumbs caressed the underside of her breasts while his lips found that place just behind her ear.

The one he knew drove her wild. "I'm sure the others can manage a night without you."

The heat radiating from his strong, masculine body was like a magical switch. He touched her, and her insides quivered with need.

It had been that way from the moment they met.

"It's only for a couple of hours." Lexi tilted her head to the side to give him better access. "To help the staff"—she moaned with approval—"survive the initial rush." As much as she hated to, Lexi brought her thoughts back into focus. Rolling her lips inward, she spread the translucent gloss before turning to face him. "I'll be back before you know it."

"Fine." Her sweet husband pretended to pout. "Text me when you're on your way?"

"Scout's honor." She held up two fingers.

Trevor's mouth curved upward and one of his dark brows arched high. "That's the Boy Scout sign, Lex."

"Oh." She chuckled before lowering her hand. "Well, you get the idea."

"Yeah, angel." He pulled her body flush with his. "I do."

Staring down at her, his brown eyes soaked her up with his heated gaze. With a slight shake of his head, he used a finger to brush a sprig of hair from her eye.

"You're absolutely stunning."

God, she loved this man. "You're not so bad, yourself."

"There is one problem with this outfit, though."

Frowning, Lexi turned to give herself a once-over in the vanity mirror. Her long, blonde hair was pulled into a half-up, half-down do. Her makeup was complete, and the simple, red dress with the capped sleeves and conservative-yet-sexy hem showed only the slightest amount of cleavage.

"What's wrong with my outfit?"

"It's not what's wrong, really," Trevor's deep voice rumbled. "More like, what's missing."

Before she could ask what he meant by that, he was reaching around her front, aligning the new necklace he'd purchased for her.

Lexi sucked in a breath as she caught sight of the delicate, silver locket. "Trev, it's beautiful!" She leaned her head forward so he could hook the clasp.

"There was an antique shop next door to my hotel. I saw this hanging in the window the first night I was there. Went straight inside and bought it."

"I love it." She caught her husband's eyes in the mirror. "Thank you."

"Open it."

Grinning, she did as he instructed. Inside was the tiniest picture of the two of them on their wedding day.

The image blurred behind unshed tears.

A soft, gentle tone caressed his voice when he spoke again. "I left the other side open. Figured, when the time comes, we can put our baby's first picture there." His lips brushed against her ear as he whispered, "And the time will come, angel.

"Oh, Trevor." She faced him again, blinking the moisture away before it could fall. "It's perfect."

He was perfect.

She wanted to give him his Valentine's Day present *so* badly. Was almost bursting at the seams to tell him. But she held back, wanting the moment to be perfect.

Because the man standing before her deserved nothing less.

Soon. You'll get to tell him, soon.

Before she blurted out the news in the middle of the bathroom, Lexi rose onto her tiptoes and kissed him softly. "Thank you."

"You're welcome." He took her mouth in his again. "Hurry back. The locket was only one part of your Valentine's surprise."

"I'll be back as soon as I can." Lexi forced herself to break free from his loving embrace.

His dark eyes burrowed into her soul, his voice filled with affection as he said, "I love you, Lex."

"I love you, too, Trevor."

With a heart so full it might explode, she turned and left, knowing the man of her dreams would be waiting for her return.

"WHAT THE FUCK DO YOU MEAN, I'M FIRED?" BRYAN MACKEY sent his piece of shit boss a nasty glare.

He'd been working his ass off for the guy, and for what...so he could be tossed out like yesterday's garbage?

"You were a no-call, no-show, Bryan. Again."

"Damn it, Todd. I *tried* to call." Bryan bit out. "Fucking cops wouldn't let me use the phone."

Todd—the owner of the construction company Bryan had been employed with for the past year—didn't seem to care. He just sat behind his desk with his hands folded in front of him.

Bastard.

"I wish the circumstances were different, Bryan. I really do. But this is your second DUI. I can't have you out driving my trucks with that kind of record."

"So I won't drive." He shrugged. "I can ride with someone else to the job sites. Darren does that shit all the time."

"Darren's been on the job less than a month. The guy's still in training." Todd shook his head. "I don't need another rider, I need someone I can count on."

"You *can* count on me!" Bryan yelled. Running a hand through hair he desperately needed to wash, he tried to convince the selfish prick to understand his situation. "Look, man. I'll do anything. Pick up scraps and trash and shit. Whatever you want, but I *need* this job. I don't keep a steady paycheck coming in, my parole officer's gonna have a shit fit. Not to mention my ex is already threatening to take me back to court for full custody. Bitch pulls that shit, I'll have nothing left."

"Well maybe you should've thought about that before you decided to tie one on and then get behind the damn wheel."

"Fuck you!" Bryan scowled at the self-righteous prick. "Like you've never stopped for a drink on your way home."

"See, the key words there are 'a drink'. You blew a point one five."

"Fine. Maybe I had a few too many, but shit. Can you blame me? I had to sit and listen to that goddamn homeowner bitch and moan about how long it was taking us. Guy wouldn't leave us alone. Just stood around, watching us all damn day. Like he even knows what it takes to build a fucking house."

"Are you even listening to yourself right now? What am I saying...of course, you're not. You're too busy blaming everyone else for the choices *you've* made." Todd stood and made his way around his desk. "Go home, Bryan. Get your shit in order, deal with your legal issues, and get your drinking under control. You do that, and maybe, in a few months, we can revisit the idea of you working here again. In the meantime, I'll mail your last paycheck as soon as it's printed."

"Fuck you and fuck this place." Bryan spun around to leave. "Never liked working for this shit company, anyway."

"You did this to yourself," Todd hollered after him. "Just remember that."

Slamming the door behind him, Bryan stormed through the building without a word to any of the other workers. He climbed into his beat-up Camry and started the ignition. Shoving the gearshift into drive, he pushed the gas pedal down as far as it would go, purposely spewing gravel behind him as he sped out of the parking lot.

"Fuck!" Steaming with anger, Bryan smacked his steering wheel.

He didn't know what he was going to do. He wasn't lying about his ex. She'd just been waiting for another opportunity to stick it to him. Now, thanks to those fucking cops and Todd firing him, she'd have it.

Bitch always did love kicking me when I was down.

An off-key ding filled the car's interior. Glancing down at the dashboard, Bryan cursed when he saw the yellow gas light shining back at him brightly.

"Fucking figures."

Christ, he was sick of living like this. He had about forty bucks to his name and was already two weeks late on his rent. For the past few days, he'd been successfully dodging his landlord's calls, but that shit wouldn't last forever.

He needed a plan. A way to come up with a decent amount of cash and fast. But first, he needed some gas.

Spotting the Quick Trip just down the road, Bryan didn't bother using his turn signal. Instead, he cut across traffic just before the gas station's entrance. The lady behind him blared her horn, but he stuck his hand out his window and flipped her the bird.

"Bitch," he mumbled under his breath.

They're all just a bunch of fucking bitches.

Pulling up to the nearest pump, he slammed the car into park. His door creaked in protest when he got out, another string of curse words running through his mind when he pulled out his wallet and noticed he had even less money than he'd thought.

With a ten in his hand, he walked inside to pre-pay. It wouldn't get him much, but he'd at least be able to get home without worrying about his car dying on the side of the road.

When the transaction was complete, the kid behind the counter thanked him and told him to have a good day.

Too late for that, dickhead.

On his way out, Bryan noticed another car had pulled up to the pump opposite his. A nicer, newer car than his. And the driver? He'd be more than happy to take *her* for a ride.

Maybe getting laid is what he needed. Sure would brighten this otherwise fucktacular day. But the closer he got, Bryan realized this woman was way the hell out of his league.

Didn't mean he couldn't enjoy the view.

You could follow her home. Invite yourself in for a little afternoon delight. Not like you have to go to work, now.

Liking the sound of that, he pulled his dark sunglasses down in order to watch the petite blonde without her knowing. Keeping his covered eyes locked on her, he went back to his own car and began unscrewing the gas cap.

Completely unaware that she was being watched, the blonde in the sexy red dress spoke on her cell phone as she inserted her debit card and began entering her PIN. Bryan listened to her conversation with deft ears.

"No, Charlie. I haven't told Trev yet. It's been *killing* me not to, but I want it to be special, you know? I have this whole thing planned out, but it'll have to wait until after I leave work."

The woman paused to listen to whatever the person on the other end of the phone call had to say.

"I know I'm the owner, but the place is going to be packed. Valentine's Day is like Black Friday for The Gardens. At least it was last year. The restaurant was filled to capacity, and the staff made a *killing* in tips. Our reservation sheet is full again this year, and we even have a waiting list in case someone calls and cancels."

Another pause.

"I'm only staying until the first big rush settles down. After that, I'm going home to spend a quiet, romantic evening with my husband. He said he has something special planned for me, too."

The blonde chuckled as she removed the pump from her car and replaced it back into its cradle.

"Right? I can't wait to see the look on his face when I give him my present. I've been really careful not to let anything slip, too." She listened to the Charlie person some more and sighed. "I promise I won't overdo it tonight."

Another long pause.

"Okay. Oh, I almost forgot...I have a special table reserved for you and Derek. I even scooted it over a smidge so you two could have a little more privacy." The blonde smiled. "I know I didn't *have* to. I wanted to. Your reservations are for seven-thirty, right? I should still be around when you guys get there. Let your server know to come get me, and I'll stop by and say hi before I leave."

There was one, final stretch of silence as the fuckable woman opened her car door and slid behind the wheel. "Sounds good. I'll see you soon." She ended the call, and pulled her door shut.

Bryan waited until she pulled out of the parking lot to remove the pump from his car. His ten dollars' worth of gas had run dry a while ago, but he'd pretended to still be filling up in order to listen to the interesting conversation.

The chick owned a restaurant. And not just any restaurant. *The Gardens.*

Bryan had never been, but his ex had always harped on him to take her there. Like he could afford a place like that.

It was located on the outskirts of town, away from the crowded downtown business. Supposedly, it was *the* restaurant in Dallas to go to—not that he could ever afford eating there.

But now, thanks to the information the blonde had just inadvertently shared, Bryan knew the place was going to be filled with rich jackasses trying to impress the women in their lives.

The staff made a killing in tips.

Bryan's shitty day just got a little brighter. With a smirk on his lips, he got into his car and started the engine. At the same time his phone began to ring.

Digging his pre-paid phone from his pocket, he saw his younger brother's number on the screen.

"What's up?"

"Where you at, man? I stopped by your work to see if you wanted to grab some lunch, but Todd said he had to let you go. Something about another DUI? What the fuck, dude?"

"Yeah, it was a bogus charge. Shawn bailed me out, though. It's no big deal."

He always could count on his childhood friend to help him out in a jam.

"No big deal? I thought you liked that job? And you were just talking the other day about how you were seriously strapped for cash. Now you've got nothing coming in at all. What the hell are you going to do?"

"Fuck that job." Bryan started his car. "Listen, do you have plans tonight?"

"Nah. Sheila and I split up again, so I was just gonna hang out at home. Maybe try to catch a game or something. Why? What's up?"

"Call Shawn. Tell him to meet us at your place in twenty."

"For what?"

Bryan thought about the pretty blonde again. He thought about the restaurant she owned and all the money her clueless customers would have shoved in their expensive pockets.

Wearing his first real smile of the day, he told his brother, "I have an idea."

2

"THIS FOOD IS to die for, Lexi," Bonnie Greer, a regular at The Gardens, smiled.

Sitting across from her, the sweet woman's husband nodded as he swallowed another bite. "The missus is right. You've really outdone yourself tonight."

"Thanks, Howard. I'm glad you're enjoying the meal."

"Always do." The gray-haired man smiled up at her. "It's why we keep coming back."

With a gentle hand on the man's suit-covered shoulder, Lexi grinned. "Just be sure to let me or one of the servers know if there's anything you need. And Happy Valentine's Day."

"It's our fifty-third one spent together." Bonnie beamed.

Lexi shook her head. "Congratulations. That's impressive."

"Especially nowadays," Bonnie commented. "These young couples...they don't know what commitment means. They go into a marriage focused on all the wrong things...the wedding, the house. Babies. They get so caught up in it all, they forget to focus on what started it all to begin with."

"Each other." Howard finished for her. He reached across the table and took his wife's hand in his.

Lexi's smile grew. "You two are very lucky."

"Well, from what I've seen..." Bonnie picked up her glass of water. "You and that handsome husband of yours are off to a good start."

"She's right,' Howard agreed. "I've seen the way you two look at each other when he's in here. It's the same way I look at my sweetie."

The loving scene had tears pricking at the corners of Lexi's eyes. It was either that or the hormones.

Probably both.

Blinking the moisture away, Lexi glanced at her watch. "Speaking of my husband, I think it's about time I head home, myself."

"You two have something special planned?"

Something very special, indeed.

"We're just going to have a quiet night at home. Between this place and his job, we're both kept pretty busy. So a night in is actually a nice treat for us."

"Enjoy, dear. You've most certainly earned it."

"Thank you. I'll let you finish your dinners. Have a wonderful evening, and be safe driving home."

Turning away from the loving couple, Lexi glanced at her watch a second time. If she left now, she shouldn't run into too much traffic.

Excitement filled her belly as she made her way to the kitchen located at the back of the restaurant. The large space was bustling with activity, the sounds and aromas mixing together in a way that always made her heart happy.

"You still here?" Maggie, the manager she'd hired a few months back, came rushing by with a piece of Lexi's infamous chocolate cake. "I thought you'd be home with that hunky hubs of yours.

Lexi grinned. "He is kind of a hunk, isn't he?"

"Kind of?" The happily married mother of three looked at

Lexi as if she'd lost her mind. "Don't get me wrong, I love my husband more than anything. But I'm pretty sure God broke the mold when He made Trevor."

She wasn't wrong.

Chuckling, Lexi reached for her coat and purse, which were both hanging on a hook next to the large walk-in freezer on her left. She usually kept her personal things in her office, but since she hadn't planned on being here very long, she'd just left them there on her way in earlier.

"As a matter of fact, I'm headed home, now. You got this covered?"

"Piece of cake." Maggie held up the plated dessert and winked. "Now, go. Spend some quality time with your man."

"Thanks, Mags. Have a good one. And call me if you need anything."

Just then, a loud clanging sound came from across the room near the sink, causing everyone to stop what they were doing and stare.

"All good, Boss," Kenny, her dishwasher, hollered. "Just a metal pan."

"Go." Maggie gave Lexi a gentle shove with her free hand. "Seriously. We'll be fine."

"I'm sure you will. And thanks, everyone!" Lexi addressed the kitchen staff. "Keep up the good work and have a great night!"

Several goodbyes and see-yas were spoken as she turned and headed for the back door. Stopping short, she gave herself one final moment to think of the tables full of happy couples enjoying the food she and her staff had prepared.

Lexi thought of Bonnie and Howard, again. She couldn't help but feel a sense of pride knowing her restaurant had brought a tiny bit of joy into their lives.

Just two short years ago, she was working at a small, run-down diner. Now she owned one of the most successful restaurants in the city.

With the help from her amazingly supportive husband, of course.

Her insides fluttered as she thought of Trevor and the news she would be sharing with him soon. After nearly a year of trying, their prayers had been answered.

They were going to have a baby.

Lexi slid a hand over her lower stomach as she made her way toward the restaurant's employee entrance. She beamed with joy and excitement, her mind becoming filled with thoughts of family and dreams come true—

"Everybody freeze!"

The loud order resonated throughout the entire restaurant...including the noisy kitchen. Several screams filled the space, and it took Lexi and the staff around her a second to realize what was happening.

Two men had just entered the building. Both were dressed in head-to-toe black—including masks—and both held up their assault rifles for everyone to see.

The taller of the two was making his way around the tables yelling at everyone to line up against the back wall and empty their pockets and purses.

"Holy shit!" Kenny dropped to the floor, hissing a hushed, "Get down!"

Everyone but Lexi immediately ducked down, out of the intruder's sights. As the owner, it was her duty to protect those in attendance.

The best way she knew to do that was to stay calm and not panic.

Easier said than done.

At least the cops would have loads of footage to go off of once this was all over. Last year, after her friend Charlie's abusive ex vandalized a truck in the parking lot out back,

Trevor had new cameras installed—both inside and out—as well as a silent alarm.

The problem was the panic button was located by the cash registers...on the opposite side of the room from where Lexi stood.

Trevor!

She wanted to call him. To hear his voice and know that everything was going to be okay.

Lexi glanced back up and saw one of the two men making his way back to the kitchen. Damn it. A phone call would be too risky.

In a split-second decision, she slid around to the far side of the large, metal shelf she was standing near. Trembling, she unzipped her purse and pulled out her phone.

Opening the messages icon, Lexi tapped Trevor's name, and as quickly as her fingers would move, she typed out the message...

Being robbed. Two men with guns. I love you!

Lexi sent it, praying he'd see the text immediately.

"Hand over the phone!"

The deep voice coming from behind her startled her. She tried turning around, but froze when the cold, hard barrel of a gun was pressed roughly against the back of her head.

"Do it, now! Unless you want me to ruin that pretty dress of yours by covering it with your brains."

Shit. She'd been so focused on sending the text, she hadn't noticed another man had entered through the back door.

At least the message sent. Trev will get help. Just like last time.

Back when she and Trevor had just started dating, a crazed man from his past began stalking her. The guy blamed Trevor for something that wasn't even his fault and ended up using her as bait to get back at him.

By the grace of God—and Trevor and the rest of R.I.S.C.'s Alpha Team—she'd survived the psychopath's attack. A lot had changed since then, but the one constant Lexi knew she could always count on was Trevor's love for her.

He'd see the text, and then he'd do whatever it took to save her and the others. Because that's who her husband was.

A hero.

A warrior.

A man who had no idea he's going to be a father.

"You've got two seconds, lady!" the man behind her warned.

Lexi's chest tightened as she thought of the tiny baby growing inside her. Instinctively, she slid the palm of her free hand over her lower belly, wishing she could do more to protect him or her.

"H-here." She held the phone out to the side. "Take it."

"Smart girl." He yanked it from her hand.

Smarter than you think, asshole.

"The rest of you," the jerk addressed the kitchen staff. "On your feet slowly and..."

Her phone began to ring.

The masked man looked at the screen and then at her. "Who's Trevor?"

"My husband." Lexi swallowed. Praying she wasn't making a horrible mistake, she looked him in his bloodshot eyes and said, "I sent him a text, so he knows you're here. If you're smart, you and your friends will leave before the cops show up."

Her phone continued to ring.

"Nice try." The guy started to put it away.

"Why would I lie about that?"

The ringing stopped.

Keeping his gun trained on her, he opened the last message she'd sent. Even from beneath the knitted ski mask, Lexi could see the muscles in his jaw flex as he read her typed words.

Dark, infuriated eyes swung back to hers. "You bitch!"

Before Lexi could react, his hand flew toward her face. Pain exploded in her cheek as his rough knuckles—and her phone —made contact. Stars burst before her eyes.

She cried out, the blow sending her flying off her feet. Her coat and purse fell away from her in opposite directions, but Lexi somehow managed to throw her hands out in front of her to break her fall.

Don't hurt the baby. Please, don't hurt my baby.

Having barely kept her midsection from slamming against the tiled floor, Lexi kept her head down and tried to regain her focus. Nausea rolled through her gut and a slow, warm trickle of blood began dripping down the side of her face.

"Hey!" Kenny shot to his feet and started for the man who'd hit her.

A deafening boom echoed off the walls, causing Lexi's ears to immediately start ringing. Muffled screams broke through the high-pitched sound, and with blurred and teary eyes, she saw Kenny's body fly backward against the sink.

Bright, crimson blood began to seep into the white material covering his left shoulder.

Oh, God!

"Kenny!" Lexi tried standing, but the man pointed his gun back in her direction.

"One more move, and you're next."

"What the fuck?" The man she'd been watching earlier came barreling through the set of swinging doors. He took in the scene, his angry eyes landing on a grimacing Kenny. "You shot him? Jesus, Shawn."

"Don't say my name, Goddamnit! We agreed, no names."

"Yeah? Well, I also said no shooting!"

"It's this bitch's fault!" The one called Shawn jutted his gun at her. "She sent a text to her fucking husband. Told him about us."

Lexi pushed herself into a sitting position and leaned against the cool, metal shelf behind her.

"That's right." She put a hand to her cheek and winced. "You should leave now. Go out that door"—she pointed to the back entrance—"and run through the trees. There's still plenty of time for you to get away."

Shawn looked at his buddy intently. "You heard her, man. The cops are coming. Let's go."

"It's not the cops you have to worry about." Lexi forced her shoulders back and her chin up. "If my husband gets to you first, you're all as good as dead."

Lexi knew that with every fiber of her being.

"I'd listen...to her." Kenny spoke through his pain. "Guy's a total...badass. Part of some... black ops...team. Works with... Homeland...Security."

Shawn snorted. "Bullshit."

Lexi hadn't planned on sharing *that* little tidbit with these idiots. But with her options as limited as they were, she decided to roll with it.

"It's true." She nodded. "My husband and his team are also very close with Dallas P.D. I guarantee you he alerted authorities the second he saw that text. The police are on their way here as we speak."

"Fuck!" Shawn yelled loudly.

The guy was antsy as all get out and clearly wanted to leave. But the other man...the one who seemed to be in charge...acted as if the cops showing up wasn't necessarily a bad thing.

Squatting down in front of her, his grey eyes stared directly into hers. "You're her." He lifted a gloved hand toward her injured face. "The one from the gas station."

Gas station?

Lexi recoiled as far as the shelf would allow, determined not to let the asshole lay a finger on her.

"I saw you there earlier today. Heard you on the phone, bragging about how busy this place was going to be. You were right." He looked over toward the large, open cutout separating the kitchen from the dining area. "I guess I should thank you."

All of the air escaped from Lexi's lungs. They were doing this because of *her*?

Forcing down the rush of bile threatening to bubble its way into her throat, she schooled her expression and jutted her chin. "You can thank me by taking your friends and getting the hell out of my restaurant."

The man's smile sent a shiver down her spine. His hand shot out, a fiery pain filling her scalp when he grabbed hold of her hair and pulled her face to his.

"You're either very brave or very stupid." He began running the end of his pistol up her thigh, sliding it beneath the hem of her dress. "Since you've got a pussy between your legs, I'm gonna go for stupid."

The guy obviously had a problem with women. No huge shock, there.

Sirens blared from somewhere nearby.

"Shit. Seriously, Bryan." Shawn paced back and forth. "They're coming. Let's *go!*"

Apparently, the no-name rule doesn't matter anymore.

Inside Lexi felt as though she was falling apart, but as scared as she was, she refused to cower down to these assholes. She had to stay strong.

For her staff.

For Trevor.

And for the new family they'd created together.

"He's right, *Bryan*," she told the man still holding onto her. "Time's running out."

"You guy's hear that?" The third man came running to the serving window. With his head on a swivel in order to keep an eye on the other hostages, he said, "The cops are almost here. I got all the wallets and phones." He held up a lumpy, weighted pillowcase. "What the hell are we waiting for?"

"Fuck this, I'm out." Shawn turned for the back door.

Bryan let her go and pointed his gun at his partner. "Take another step and I blow a hole through your spine."

Shawn turned back around. "Really? What are you gonna do? Shoot me for trying to keep my ass from getting arrested?"

"It's too late." Bryan pointed to the air and tilted his head. "Hear that? They're already on us."

Shawn began to panic even more. With his hands holding the sides of his head, he began pacing back and forth like a wild man.

"Shit... Fuck... *Shit!*" The shelf behind Lexi shook from the force of Shawn's hand smacking against it.

"Dude, chill," Bryan muttered. "It's going to be fine."

"Fine?" The man's voice rose an octave. His eyes widened as they slid to something behind Bryan. "Look outside, asshole. We're about as far from fucking fine as you can get."

The third guy, who was still at the window, turned around to see whatever it was Shawn was talking about. "Ah, hell. There are so many lights it's like freaking Christmas!"

"What do we do now?" Shawn looked to Bryan for direction.

The police are here.

It was a wonderful thing...and a horrible thing.

If the cops were present, then they for sure knew of the situation. But they most likely had the place surrounded, which meant these guys would either have to surrender or...

Bryan doesn't seem like the surrendering type.

Lexi let out a slow breath. Damn it. Why didn't the idiots leave when they had the chance?

This is your fault. If you hadn't texted Trevor, they'd probably be gone by now. Kenny wouldn't have been shot, and you wouldn't be sitting here with a throbbing headache from getting clocked with your own phone.

No. She couldn't allow herself to believe that. Texting Trevor was the exact right thing to do.

This was her restaurant. These people were her responsibility. And after what she went through a couple of years ago, Lexi had promised herself she'd never be a victim again.

It's why she'd stood up to Shawn the way she had. She thought maybe if the jerks knew about the text, they'd get scared and leave.

Instead, she'd put her staff at even more risk. She'd put herself and her *baby* at risk. Kenny had been shot, and now they were all stuck here with these three maniacs.

I'm sorry, Trev. I'm so, so sorry.

"Bry!" Shawn shoved at Bryan's shoulder. "Are you even listening to me, man?"

Slowly, Bryan stood. Using his teeth, he removed one of his gloves.

"Give me the phone." He let the glove drop and held out his hand.

Shawn handed Bryan her phone. "What's the plan?"

"We're going to make a list. After that, we're gonna make a phone call."

"A phone call?"

Bryan nodded. "If this bitch's husband is who they say he is, then he's got enough connections to get us a shit ton more money than what's in those wallets. He can also arrange for a ride out of here."

Shawn looked back at his partner in disbelief. "Do you even hear yourself? Jesus!"

"He's right, Bry," the man at the window sided with Shawn. "Maybe we should just—"

"Maybe you two should shut your mouths and do what I say!" Bryan bellowed. "I'm in charge, remember? This whole plan was *mine*, so unless you want to give up your cuts, I suggest you stop your whining and get back to watching the hostages.

And pick two of them to close the blinds on all the windows so the cops can't see inside."

Lexi sucked in a silent breath. She wondered if the guy even realized what he'd just said.

Bryan had just confessed to planning the robbery. She heard it, the kitchen staff heard it, and the cameras most likely picked it up, too.

If the dumbass makes it out of this thing alive, he's going to be so screwed.

Bryan and the other guy began discussing demands. They argued back and forth for what felt like hours before coming up with ones they both agreed on. When they were finally finished, he used the notes app on her phone to type out a list of demands.

With his cold, arrogant eyes locked with hers, Bryan held the phone up so she could see he'd found Trevor's number in her contacts. His lips curled into an eerie smile.

"Time to call your hubby."

3

Trevor's eyes were glued to Lexi's building. Utterly helpless, he watched while two women—presumably hostages—dropped the blinds on all of the windows.

His insides shook, and he felt like he was going to puke while he waited for the police to decide on their next move.

It had been over half an hour since he'd gotten the text alerting him of the robbery, and he hadn't been able to take a full breath since.

Please don't take her from me.

There was only one other time in his life when he'd felt this same, soul-consuming fear. Two years ago, when Lexi had been kidnapped and nearly killed.

Thankfully he and his team found her just in time. They'd saved her, and as a bonus, Trevor had taken out the man who'd dared to touch what was his. That shit still gave him nightmares.

He'd vowed that day to never let that sort of danger come near her again. Yet here he was, standing with his thumb up his ass while his wife—his *life*—was inside with those bastards.

"Let me go in." He turned to the man standing to his right.

"My team should be on their way, and you know we don't travel light."

Meaning they all carried weapons and other tactical gear in their personal vehicles. You never knew when the occasion may arise where it was needed.

This sure as hell qualifies.

Looking official in his black slacks, white button-up, and DPD ballistics vest, Detective Eric West was the twin brother to Derek West, one of Trevor's teammates.

He was also a friend.

"You know I can't do that." Eric stared back at him, his expression a mixture of frustration and pity.

"Bullshit." Trevor growled. "You're the detective in charge."

With his hands on his hips, Eric shifted his body to face him more directly. "That's right. I *am* in charge, which means I have to follow department procedure. That means I can't allow a civilian to voluntarily walk into a hostage situation."

"I'm not a civilian!" Trevor shouted. Okay, so technically he was, but *fuck*. "My team and I have more training and experience with hostage rescue missions than any HRT the Dallas PD has on their payroll."

The department's Hostage Rescue Team was probably damn good at its job, but this was his *wife* they were talking about. Still, Eric didn't back down.

"You already told me the place was going to be packed tonight, which means there are a helluva lot of lives resting in my hands right now. If I let you and your team go in and something goes sideways, that shit's on me." Eric ran a hand over the stubble covering his jaw. "I'm sorry, Trev, but until we know more about what we're dealing with, I can't send anyone in."

Pinpricks of fear and frustration stabbed at every last nerve in Trevor's body.

"We know *exactly* what's going on in there." He held up his phone so Eric could see the text again. "Lexi *told* us. Two HT's.

Two, Eric. You know Alpha Team can take 'em. Hell, I could take them myself."

"But at what cost?" Riley, Eric's partner, walked toward them. The attractive woman's long, dark hair was slicked back in a flawless ponytail that swished from side to side as she moved. "You take one hostage-taker out, the other could start shooting innocent civilians. We could lose a lot of lives before you're able to put one of your bullets in the bastard."

On the verge of losing his temper completely, Trevor kept his voice steady, but firm. "I won't give him the chance to shoot."

Riley seemed to be considering this, but the same pity he'd seen in Eric's eyes a minute before reflected back at him through hers.

"You're too close to this thing, Trevor." She held onto the upper straps of her vest. "If you weren't, you'd know we're doing everything we can to make sure everyone, including Lexi, gets out of this thing unscathed."

They're not fucking listening!

"What if it was Charlie in there?" Trevor turned back to Eric. "You really going to stand there and tell me you'd be sitting around, waiting for the HT's to make their move if that was your sister-in-law in there?"

"Fuck no, he wouldn't."

Speak of the devil.

All eyes turned to see Derek and Charlie—the sister-in-law in question—approaching the yellow barricade the police had erected to keep the public back. He pointed to the tape and waited for his brother to give them permission to cross under and join them.

Though he looked more like a West Coast surfer, Derek was a former SEAL and Alpha Team's genius tech wizard. He was also the group's class clown.

The guy was always wearing dumbass t-shirts and cracking

jokes but not tonight. Tonight he was dressed in a suit and tie, and his usual playful attitude was nowhere to be seen.

"Hey, man." He went straight up to Trevor and half-hugged him. "We were just gettin' ready to leave the house to come here for dinner when Jake called."

Derek's southern accent was thicker than normal, which told Trevor the guy was as pissed—and worried—as he was.

"Good thing you made reservations for later in the evening, or you'd be in there, too." Eric commented to his brother.

"Trust me." Derek pulled Charlie a little closer. "I've already thought of that."

Like Trevor, there was nothing more important to Derek than keeping the woman he loved safe.

"The others coming?" Trevor asked despite already knowing the answer.

His team had his back. Always.

Derek nodded. "Jake and Liv were stayin' at some swanky hotel in Houston, but they're headed this way. So is Mike. He said he'd get ahold of Coop and Mac, and I left a message for Grant. Everyone should be here soon."

"Thanks, D." Trevor slapped the guy's back. "Appreciate it."

"What about Lexi?" A very worried Charlie looked to Trevor. "Have you talked to her? Is she okay?"

Trevor shook his head. "I've tried calling a bunch of times, but it keeps getting sent to voicemail."

Charlie crossed her arms in front of her chest as if to hug herself. Trevor knew she was scared for Lexi. They all were.

His wife was close to the whole Alpha Team family, but Lexi and Charlie had a special bond. One that formed the moment Derek had introduced them. The two met, and they'd been best friends ever since.

"Like Riley said." Eric spoke up again. "We're doing every-thing we can to get Lex and the others out safely."

Trevor's angered gaze shifted to Derek's. "And by everything, your brother means we're out here while my wife is in there, being held at fucking gunpoint."

"Have there been any demands?"

"None." Trevor shook his head. "Cops tried calling the land-line inside, but the assholes refused to pick up."

His fists tightened at his sides, and anger stirred to the point he wanted to punch someone. Better yet, he wanted to *shoot* someone.

The longer they waited to take action, the longer Lexi was at risk of being hurt. Or worse.

Don't go there, man. You've got to stay positive. For her.

"What's the plan, Eric?" Derek turned to his brother, his voice low and controlled. Like Trevor, he was in total operator mode.

Eric looked at his watch. "We give them five more minutes to make contact, and then—"

Trevor started to erupt, but Eric raised a hand and stopped him.

"And *then*"—the detective continued—"we send SWAT in to smoke them out."

"Smoke them out?" Charlie frowned. "What does that mean?"

Derek took his wife's hand. "It means they'll shoot cans of tear gas through the windows before breachin' the structure."

"Tear gas?" She blinked. "Will that hurt the baby?"

The men all shared a confused look.

"Baby?" Eric turned to her. "There's a kid inside? I thought the place was full of couples celebrating Valentine's Day."

Charlie's eyes widened slightly. Her face filled with an embarrassing blush as she began stumbling over her words. "No! I mean, uh...I-I don't know. I just meant that *if* there was a baby...or...a pregnant woman inside...would tear gas be harmful to them?"

Trevor studied his wife's friend closely. She was suddenly

making eye contact with everyone but him, which was odd, but he was too focused on Lexi to worry about it.

"CS is the most commonly used component," he quickly explained. "The gas causes watery eyes, a runny nose, coughing...that sort of thing. But unless someone is exposed to it for a prolonged period of time, the effects are usually harmless and clear up within half an hour or so."

"Oh." Charlie smiled. "Good." Then the strange-acting woman pulled on her husband's hand and said, "Can I talk to you for a second?"

As the two moved a few feet away for their intense-looking conversation, a twenty-something cop approached Eric and Riley.

"Sorry to interrupt, Detectives, but I have some information I thought you'd want to know."

Riley nodded. "What it is, Officer Wilmes?"

"We just got word from a resident living nearby that a gunshot was fired at this location. It was reported a few minutes before we arrived on the scene."

"Gunshot?" Trevor's heart flew into his throat. Without warning, the image of Lexi bleeding out flashed through his mind. *Oh, Jesus.* He looked at Eric. "We have to get inside."

Eric thanked the officer, who took his cue and left. Running a hand through his already mussed hair, he said, "Look, Trev. I understand how you feel, but we still can't—"

"No." Trevor's voice lowered. "You don't." With a deadly calm, he got right into the other man's face. "Until it's *your* woman in there...one you'd die for...one you can't imagine living a single *day* without..." His voice cracked, and he had to clear his throat before continuing on. "Until that day comes, you can't even *begin* to know what I'm fucking feeling."

In an almost indiscernible move, Eric's gaze slid toward Riley. For a split second, Trevor could've sworn he saw a familiar emotion there—the same one a man had when he looked at the woman he loved.

But then Eric blinked, and it was gone.

"I didn't mean—" Eric started to explain, but Riley put a hand on his shoulder and gently pulled him back.

"Let's all take a deep breath," she suggested just as Trevor's phone began to ring.

He pulled it from his pocket, the air in his lungs freezing when he saw the screen.

"It's Lexi!" he practically shouted, holding it up for the others to see. "It's her!"

"Wait!" Eric stopped him from tapping the screen. "Don't answer it yet." Moving at warp speed, he opened a recording app on his own phone. "Okay. Put it on speaker."

"Lexi?" Trevor answered, not bothering to hide his concern. "Baby, are you okay?"

But the gravelly voice that came on the line wasn't hers. "Ah, ain't that sweet?"

Raw anger shot through him. "Let me talk to my wife."

"You don't give the orders here, pal," the asshole responded. "That would be me."

"And you would be?"

"Don't worry about my fucking name, dipshit. You just do as you're told, and we'll all be on our merry way."

Trevor ground his teeth together. He and his team had witnessed this game a hundred times. They'd go back and forth with demands and denials until either the hostage takers got tired and gave up, or the cops decided to go in.

In the meantime, he and the others had no choice but to play nicey-nice with a bunch of thugs. Because that's how the game is played.

Trevor hated the fucking game.

"What do you want?" he asked with a calm he most definitely did not feel.

"I want you to show me some goddamn respect."

And I want to kill you.

He'd dealt with assholes like him before. Guys who thought everyone was out to get them. Ones who believed the world owed them some huge debt they hadn't even come close to earning.

As much as it burned his ass, Trevor knew he'd have to stroke the guy's ego if he wanted this thing to end peacefully.

"You've got it," Trevor went along with the bullshit while the others hovered quietly around the outstretched phone. "What else?"

"We have a list of demands. I know what you do for a living, *Trevor*, so don't bother trying to bullshit me on this. I want everything on the list ready to go within the hour, or we start shooting the hostages. Starting with your pretty little wife."

I'm going *to kill you.*

"I'll pull whatever strings I have to in order to help you out," Trevor assured him. "But I need something from you, first."

It didn't matter what these assholes wanted. If it meant having Lexi back in his arms, Trevor would make damn sure they got it. And then he was going to end them.

"Yeah?" The arrogant prick asked. "What's that?"

"I need to talk to Lexi. Make sure she's all right."

The pause that followed nearly drove Trevor mad. But then...

"Trev?"

"Lex?" He blew out a breath, nearly falling to his knees with relief. "Oh, thank God. Are you okay? Did they hurt you?"

"I-I'm fine, but Trev...Kenny was shot. Left shoulder. The bullet went straight through, and the bleeding seems to be slowing down some, but he needs help. Soon."

Damn. Kenny was a nice guy and a hard worker. He sure as shit didn't deserve to be caught up in this mess.

No one in there did.

With his eyes bouncing between Eric and Riley, Trevor nodded. "Okay, sweetheart. I'll work on that."

"They want me to read the list of demands to you." She spoke quickly. "These are things that Bryan, Shawn, and the one other guy wanted you to... *Ah!*"

Lexi cried out. The sound of flesh hitting flesh filled the speaker, followed by a shuffle.

"Try that shit again, bitch," the man who'd been speaking to Trevor warned Lexi. "See what happens."

The man went on to recite the list of demands, himself, but Trevor barely heard a word that was said.

His blood had turned to acid, the molten rage building up inside him threatening to overtake him. The bastard had hit Lexi. He knew it, and from the pissed off expressions on the others' faces, they knew it, too.

However, thanks to the brave move his wife had taken, they now also knew that there were *three* guys inside. Not two, as they'd originally thought.

Don't risk yourself anymore, baby. Please.

"That's it." The guy's voice broke through Trevor's thoughts. "Those are the demands."

With the phone held so tightly he thought it might shatter, Trevor warned the bastard, "Touch her again, and I'll kill you."

The cocky fuck seemed unfazed. "Clock's a-tickin', *Trev*. Better get to working on that list."

And then, the line went dead.

The bastard clearly didn't take the threat to his life seriously. A mistake that would cost him dearly.

"Okay, so we've got a list." Riley held up the pad of paper she'd written the demands on as the HT had recited them.

Good thing someone was listening.

"It's not much"—she looked up at him—"But it's a start."

"Fuck the list." Trevor shot her a look. "And fuck procedure. I know the building. Hell, I helped *design* the damn thing.

There's a secured emergency exit hatch directly above Lex's office. I can use that to—"

"You heard what the guy said, Trev." Riley tried calming him. "We only have an hour to meet these demands, or he's going to kill your wife."

"*Exactly!*" He urged them to listen. God, he couldn't *breathe* for how terrified he was. "You two start working on the demands, and in the meantime, I have"—he glanced at Derek — "*we* have an hour to get inside and end this thing."

"He's right, Eric." Derek gave his brother a pleading look. "We need to get Lexi out of there. Now."

"Jesus, you two don't listen for shit." Eric raked his fingers through his hair. "We have the list. That means we can start *negotiating*. Worst case, SWAT is still on standby waiting for my order to hit them with the tear gas if they don't—"

"Wrong." Trevor cut him off. "Worst case, my wife gets shot because we're too busy playing by the fucking *rules!*"

"This isn't a R.I.S.C. op, Trevor!" Eric blasted back. "I have to follow proced—"

"She's pregnant!" Charlie blurted suddenly, causing everyone in the vicinity to stop talking and stare.

Riley's dark brows turned inward. "What?"

"Who's pregnant?" Trevor and Eric both asked in unison.

"Lexi. She wanted it to be a surprise." Charlie's delicate shoulders fell. Tears filled her eyes as they rose to meet his. "She was going to tell you tonight, after she left work. But then..." Her voice cracked, and she swiped at a tear. "Damn it, I swore I wouldn't say anything. And I wouldn't have, but if you're really going to toss tear gas or whatever through the windows with her inside, I thought you needed to know."

Trevor blinked. Had he heard right? "Lexi's...*pregnant*?"

Holy shit. He could barely let himself even *think* the word for fear he'd misunderstood.

They'd been trying for nearly a year, with no success. Every month they hoped and waited, but it hadn't happened for them. Not yet.

Trevor wanted nothing more than to give Lex the family he knew she'd always wanted. The family they *both* wanted. And now...

We're having a baby?

"It's early yet," Charlie explained. "She's only about five weeks give or take. I'm sorry I blurted it out like that. I just didn't want the cops filling the place with a bunch of chemicals without you knowing."

Still stunned by the news, Trevor shook his head in awe. "I'm going to be a father."

Derek grabbed his shoulder and squeezed. "That's what Lexi was tellin' me when she pulled me away. I didn't say anything before, because I didn't want to worry you even more than you already are, but...congratulations, man."

The others around him took a moment to wish him the same, but Trevor was suddenly too busy planning to hear them.

With renewed determination rolling through him like a powerful storm, he knew exactly what he had to do.

Locking eyes with Eric, he said, "I respect you and our friendship. I also respect the position you're in, so I won't insult you by going behind your back."

"What the hell does that mean?" Eric scowled.

"It means, I'm done waiting." He slid Derek a sideways glance. "You got your tablet with you?"

"You have to ask?" The man thumbed toward the parking lot behind him. "It's in the car."

"Good. I need you to access the building's security system. Be my eyes and ears while I go inside." Trevor paused. "That is, if you're with me on this."

Derek looked genuinely insulted. "Hell yeah, I'm with you."

Tipping his chin in thanks, Trevor pointed to Eric's vest. "Mind if I borrow that?"

A moment passed between the two men, and for a second he thought the other man was going to continue standing in his way. But then Eric muttered a curse and began pulling the vest's Velcro straps free.

"Fine, dickhead." He removed the protective barrier. "But if there are holes in this when I get it back, I'm gonna be pissed."

Despite the situation, Trevor felt his mouth curl into a smirk. "Ah, you *do* care."

"Fuck off." Eric smacked the vest against his chest. "And for Christ's sake, don't do anything stupid like get yourself killed."

Trevor slid the weighted vest over his head and secured it in place. In the back of his mind, he thought about what he'd just learned. Part of him—a huge freaking part—wanted to jump up and cheer at the news that he and Lex were having a baby. But now wasn't the time.

As with any op, he needed to keep his head on straight and focus on the mission. Except this wasn't just *any* op. And God forbid he was wrong about this, his decision could end up costing him everything.

4

LEXI KEPT pressure on Kenny's wound. After ending the call with Trevor, she'd finally talked Bryan into letting her come over to help by reminding him that if Kenny died during the commission of a robbery—one Bryan had admitted to planning —then all three men would be charged with murder.

He'd also ordered Shawn to join the third man in the dining area to help keep an eye on the people out front. Since that time, she and the others in the kitchen had just been sitting. Waiting.

Praying.

"Ah!" Kenny winced when Lexi pressed a little too hard.

"Sorry," she apologized softly. Ignoring the blood covering her hands and the pounding in her head, she stared back at her employee and friend. "This is all my fault."

His expression turned incredulous. "These guys are assholes, Boss. That has nothing to do with you."

Lexi appreciated the thought, but she knew better. "You heard what he said, Kenny. The only reason they came here tonight was because he heard *me* on the phone with Charlie."

He was shaking his head before she'd even finished talking.

"And if they hadn't chosen this place, it would've been some other business."

Selfishly, she wished they *had* chosen another place to rob. Which probably made her a horrible, awful person.

At least my baby would be safe.

Regret flooded her veins as she thought of the tiny human growing inside her. The longer they were forced to sit here, the more time she'd had to think. About a million thoughts had crossed through her mind, but the one that stood out the most was that she should've told Trevor she was pregnant.

Despite her good intentions, Lexi was convinced that keeping the news a secret from Trevor had been a mistake.

They both understood—more than most—that life could change with a single heartbeat. Tomorrows were never a guarantee, and everyone should grasp each day and hold on tight... as if it were their last.

Normally, that's the way she and Trev approached each day, but with news like this...damn, it, with *this*, she'd wanted the night to be one they'd never forget.

Careful what you wish for.

Lexi released a heavy sigh. She'd really screwed the pooch on this one, and the list of mistakes seemed endless.

Not telling her sweet husband she was expecting. Letting some random piece of garbage hear her talking about what a killing this place would make tonight. Not protecting her staff the way she should have.

"Would you stop?"

Her eyes flew up to find Kenny staring back at her. "Stop what?"

"You're still blaming yourself for this shit, and you need to knock it off."

In spite of the fear and heartache she felt, Lexi let her mouth spread into a hint of a smile. "You giving me orders,

Kenneth? Because last I checked, I sign your checks. Not the other way around."

"Yeah, well." He grimaced. "This hole in my shoulder should give me a free pass tonight. Don't ya think?"

Her smile fell flat as the weight of the situation pressed back down onto her shoulders.

"Ah, hell, Boss. I didn't mean—" Kenny stopped himself short. He looked up, toward the ceiling and waited.

"What?" Lexi followed his line of sight.

"You hear that?"

She listened closely for a few seconds before shaking her head. "I don't hear anythi—"

A slight shuffling sound reached her ears. It was so faint she barely heard it, but it was there. Right above where she and Kenny sat.

"There!" he spoke with a hushed whisper. "I *know* you heard it that time."

"Yeah." Lexi nodded. "I did."

Though she couldn't be sure, but it almost sounded like someone was on the roof.

The police? Trevor? Or maybe there was a fourth guy standing guard up there in case the cops tried to enter.

When they heard the sound again, Lexi became convinced it wasn't another robber. The person moving above them was being too quiet. Too cautious.

Because they don't want Bryan and the others to know they're there.

"They're coming in," she told Kenny quietly.

"About damn time."

"Agreed," she chuckled. She just prayed things wouldn't get worse before they got better.

"What the fuck's so funny?" Bryan growled as he walked over to them.

Lexi didn't bother looking at him when she spoke. "Nothing."

"No? Because it sure sounded like something to me."

Go away, douchebag.

"I told her a dumb joke," Kenny lied. "That's all."

"Yeah? Why don't you tell it to me?"

Kenny slid her a quick glance before looking up at Bryan. "It's really not that funny."

"Did I ask if it was funny, shithead? No. I asked you to tell me the fucking joke." Bryan kicked his booted toe into Kenny's side, causing Kenny to cry out in pain.

"Stop it!" Lexi shot to her feet, putting herself between the two men. "He didn't do anything to you, so why don't you just go back over there and let us be?"

The guy had already proven he didn't like being stood up to, but she didn't care.

Kenny was her employee. Her friend. Her responsibility. And she refused to stand idly by and watch this asshole hurt him more than he already had.

"My, my, my..." Bryan smirked. "Boss Lady grew some balls."

"I've got more balls than you'll ever have."

The words were out of her mouth before she could stop them, but that didn't make them any less true.

"That so?" Bryan snarled. Using his free hand, he grabbed hold of her upper arm and pulled her body flush with his. "How about you prove it."

"Leave her alone!" Kenny hollered from his place on the floor.

The rest of the kitchen staff watched in silent fear as Bryan's cold, gray eyes fell onto Kenny. Then, in a surprising move, he used the hand holding the gun to pull off his ski mask, revealing his face for all to see.

The first thought Lexi had was that he was an unremarkable man. Not attractive, but not really *un*attractive, either.

His light brown hair was a bit too long and mussed from the cap. His eyes made her think he was in his late-twenties, maybe early thirties, but the lines on his face and the stubble covering his chin made him look deceptively older.

To her, Bryan looked like someone most people would pass by on the street and not even notice.

Maybe that's why he's doing this. To get noticed.

He started pulling her toward the back of the room and around the corner, to her office.

"Stop! What are you doing?" Lexi tried—and failed—to free herself from his painful grasp.

"I'm thinking you need a reminder of who's in charge, here."

Fear spike through her, pricking her insides like a million tiny knives. "Let go of me!"

Determined not to disappear around that corner, she tried digging in her heels. But since she was literally *in* heels, the only thing Lexi managed to do was slip and lose her footing.

She started to fall, but Bryan kept his hold. He yanked her back to her feet with such force, she thought her shoulder was going to pop out of place.

Shit that hurt!

"Please!" Lexi grasped at the shelves. The wall. Anything within reach to keep her from moving even an inch farther. "I'm pregnant!"

"Yeah, right." Bryan snorted. "Do I look that stupid to you?"

Uh, yeah...you do.

"You bitches are all the same." Bryan stopped walking long enough to spew his hateful words. "You want, want, want, but the second things don't go your way, you turn into manipulating cunts."

"Bryan!" The youngest of the three hollered through the kitchen window. "What the hell are you doing?"

"Showing this bitch what it feels like to be used up and spit out."

"Please." Lexi shot the other guy a frantic look. "Don't let him do this."

He glanced back at her with an expression of shock and pity but ignored her and continued talking to his partner. "Dude, our deadline's almost up. The cops are gonna be calling with our shit, so we need to be ready, and...fuck. You took off your mask?"

"Shut the hell up, little brother," Bryan ordered. "Just keep an eye on this bunch and let me worry about watching the time."

Little brother.

So that's who the third man was.

Lexi was locking that information away for later when Bryan started walking again.

"Seriously, man." His brother tried getting through to him again. "Is that really necessary?"

Bryan stopped again, this time so quickly Lexi slammed against his back. Swinging them both around, he stared back at his brother. "Have I ever let you down?"

The other man licked his nervous lips and shook his head. "No."

"That's right, I haven't. And I'm not about to start, now. So do me a favor and watch the kitchen while I take care of my other...business. Trust me." He smiled down at Lexi. "This won't take long."

Bryan was too busy arguing with his brother to notice another round of shuffling above them.

Please, God. Please *let that be someone coming to help us.*

5

TREVOR TREAD CAREFULLY ACROSS THE GARDENS' roof. He needed to move as quickly as possible while making as little *noise* as possible. Thanks to his Delta days, he was an expert at doing just that.

"D, you read me?" he asked through the coms he and Derek both had with their other portable gear.

"Loud and clear, brother."

The pressure in his chest eased slightly. Entering a situation without physical back-up wasn't ideal, but he wasn't about to wait on the others to arrive before going in.

Knowing Derek was able to see and hear what was happening inside allowed him to focus on the task at hand.

"You have a visual yet?"

"Affirmative. Looks like the customers are all sittin' up against the dining area's far west wall. There are two men on them, weapons in hand. Look to be AR-15s. Both have bulging pockets, so I'm guessin' they have extra mags, as well."

He had to ask. "Any sign of Lexi?"

"Negative."

"Try the kitchen."

He *needed* to know she was okay. It had been far too long since he'd talked to her, and it took every ounce of training Trevor had not to let himself imagine a bunch of worst-case scenarios.

"Switching camera views, now." There was a slight pause and then, "I've got her. Lex is in the kitchen, squatted down by the sink. She's holdin' pressure on that Kenny's guy's shoulder. I can't make out what they're sayin', but they seem to be doin' okay. Scared, but okay."

Thank Christ.

Trevor closed his eyes and hung his head. Drawing in a calming breath, he took a few precious seconds to regroup before continuing on.

"I should be moving directly over them right about now."

The plan was for him to get inside by using the roof access he'd had installed when the building was constructed. Lexi had insisted on having her private office in the back, near the kitchen. That way if her staff needed her, she'd be close by.

Trevor had argued that it wasn't safe because if a fire broke out in the kitchen while she was working in her office, it could potentially block the building's back exit, and she'd be trapped.

So they'd compromised by having a galvanized roof hatch with a folding staircase installed directly above her office.

"Hold up!" Derek warned.

Trevor froze. "What is it?"

"Pretty sure Lexi just heard you."

That's right, baby. I'm coming for you.

"Okay, I think you're clear. Ghost steps, man."

"Copy that."

He'd only taken a few more steps when Derek's voice came through the coms again. "Shit. Not sure what set him off, but our guy's pissed. He's yelling at Lexi, and...ah, hell."

"What?"

"He just took off his mask."

Damn it.

Revealing his face to the hostages could mean one of two things. The HT with Lexi was either so arrogant he didn't think it mattered, or the son of a bitch didn't plan on leaving any witnesses behind to ID him. No matter which way you went, it wasn't good news.

Except...

"Can you run facial rec?"

"Already on it." There was a slight pause and then, "Fuck! Trev, you need to get your ass in there. Now."

His chest tightened. "SITREP."

"Prick just grabbed Lex. He's pullin' her toward the back. She's tryin' to fight him off, but he's got at least a hundred pounds on her. Looks like he's tryin' to take her to her office. Goddamnit!"

Son of a...

Trevor pulled his weapon—one equipped with a military-grade suppressor—from his

waistband. He double-checked the chamber to make sure it housed a round.

Moving as quietly as he could, he covered the remaining distance to the metal hatch with precision and ease.

Entering the code only he, Lexi, and a few select employees knew, Trevor's patience was paper thin waiting for the red light on the security keypad to turn green. The second it did, he lifted the hatch, being careful not to go too fast and give his position away. He began pushing against the folding metal staircase.

Once the hydraulics kicked in, he waited until it was mostly unfolded to begin his descent into Lexi's office. He was halfway down the steps when he heard her terrified voice.

"Please. Don't let him do this!"

Derek spoke again. "Fuck. They're comin' your way!"

No shit!

Trevor pushed away his anger and focused. "I've got this, D. Keep an eye out front and wait for my order."

Trusting in what he said, Derek went radio silent. Because that's what his team did. They trusted one another.

A familiar voice traveled through the office walls.

"Shut the hell up, little brother. Just keep an eye on this bunch and let me worry about watching the time."

So at least two of the three HT's are brothers. Duly noted.

Knowing the man had his hands on Lexi again—he'd warned him about that shit—Trevor's insides burned with the need to kill. But despite his desire to end the bastard, he somehow managed to keep his shit together in order to do what needed to be done.

Climbing the rest of the way down, he chose to lift the metal staircase back up to avoid suspicion when the asshole came into the room. Thankfully, the state-of-the-art set-up was nearly silent in its movements.

Using the long, wooden rod Lexi kept over in the corner, he hooked the loop on the inner hatch and shoved it closed. Quickly, Trevor then replaced the rod and positioned himself behind the office door.

Triple checking his weapon, he took a few seconds to steady his breathing. It wasn't easy given what was at stake. Was even *harder* when the bastard who had Lexi uttered his next, chilling words.

"So do me a favor and watch the kitchen while I take care of my other...business. Trust me, this won't take long."

No, dickhead. It sure won't.

Trevor's teeth ground painfully together, his need to kill causing his trigger finger to twitch. He had a pretty good idea what the son of a bitch was planning to do to Lexi, but Trevor would have to be dead before he ever let that happen.

And he had no plans of dying anytime soon.

Footfalls reached his ear through the wall. He listened to

the man's smug, sure-of-himself stomps, using those and the quick clicks of Lexi's heels to prepare for action.

It wasn't easy, keeping a cool head. Not when his rage was a living, breathing thing.

Though he may have looked in complete control, Trevor's insides shook as he fought against the primal need to protect his wife and child. It took *everything* he had not fling the door open and fill the prick full of holes.

Soon, Matthews. You'll get your chance very soon.

Once again, Trevor called upon his training to remain still and silent. When the footsteps got closer, he blocked out Lexi's unanswered pleas and held his breath.

Then he waited.

The door flew open. The man pushed Lexi inside with such force, she fell to her hands and knees. *Fucker.*

His target stepped inside, the man's focus one hundred percent on Lexi. "You've been a pain in my ass all fucking night." His arm shifted as he swung his gun in her direction.

To control her? Shoot her? Either way, Trevor couldn't take the chance. Not when it came to his wife and child.

He aimed his weapon and pulled the trigger. The single, near-silent shot instantly severing the man's spinal cord at the base of his neck.

The asshole dropped where he stood.

Lexi screamed, scrambling back to avoid the body. Confusion and shock fell over her face, but then her eyes rose to his, and he knew she understood.

Without a word, Trevor shoved his gun into his waistband and went to her.

"Alexis!" Her full name fell from his lips.

"Trevor?" she sobbed. His wife reached for him.

With emotion clogging his throat, he pulled her to her feet and held her close. Kissing the top of her head, he let his lips linger there as he squeezed his eyes shut and sent up his own silent prayer of thanks.

"I th-thought..." Her breath hitched. "He was going t-to..."

"Shh...I know, baby." He rested his cheek against her silky hair. "I know. He can't hurt you or anyone else, ever again."

She lifted her head, the most beautiful set of red-rimmed eyes searching his. "Is it over? Can we go home, now?"

"Almost." Through his mic, he spoke to Derek again. "Target one is down, Derek."

"I heard," Derek replied immediately. "Nice work, brother."

"Status?"

"The other two are still in the dining area, oblivious to what just went down."

"Good." Trevor nodded. "Send them in."

There was a slight pause before Derek asked, "You don't want the honors?"

"No." Trevor looked down at his wife. "I'm right where I need to be."

Because if all hell broke loose, he would be putting himself between her and anyone who dared come through that door.

"Copy that. Sendin' in the troops, now."

Lexi blinked away more tears. "What's going on?"

"SWAT's securing the other two targets."

Right on cue, the sound of glass shattering, women screaming, and men yelling erupted from the front of the restaurant. Thankfully, there wasn't any gunfire.

Lexi's entire body tensed. "Do you need to go?"

Trevor shook his head. Cupping her face, he stared into her baby blues, thanking God once more that he had the opportunity to do so.

The bruises and scratch on her face, along with the angry marks on her arm, made him wish he could kill every single one of the bastards. But his relief that she was alive and seemingly okay overshadowed his need for revenge.

"I love you so much, Alexis." He leaned in for a kiss before pulling back and placing his hand over her lower belly. "I love you both."

She sucked in a breath and her eyes grew wide. "You knew?"

"Not until tonight. Charlie let it slip, but don't be mad." He quickly added. "There was talk of SWAT storming the place, and she was afraid the tear gas would harm the baby."

"I'm not mad." Lexi smiled. "I thought everything needed to be perfect, but I was wrong. When those men stormed in here tonight, I realized it didn't matter when or how I told you. The moment would be perfect because *we*'re what make moments like that perfect. You and me. Together."

God, he loved this woman.

"I love you, angel" he decided she needed to hear the words, again.

"I love you, too, Trevor."

He kissed her again. They were *still* kissing when someone cleared their throat from behind him.

"Sorry to interrupt, but I thought you'd want to know...the building's secure."

He turned and saw Eric standing in the doorway. "The other two targets?"

"In custody."

The two men shared a solemn nod.

Tilting his head to the side Eric offered Lexi a genuine smile. "Hey, Lex. Damn glad to see you're okay." Glancing down at the body lying near Trevor's feet, he shook his head. "This guy, on the other hand..."

"That's Bryan." Lexi stared at the body with disgust. "He planned this whole thing. Even admitted it out loud, so it should be on the security footage."

Trevor turned to his wife. His eyes fell to the cut on her face. "He the one who did that?"

He wanted to shoot the bastard again.

"No." Lexi's fingertips went to the worst of her injuries. "That was Shawn. He was mad because I'd texted you."

His jaw clenched, and he swung his gaze back to Eric's.

"Don't worry." The other man seemed to read his thoughts. "I'll personally oversee his booking. In the meantime"—he drew in a deep breath and let it out—"I'll need a formal statement from the both of you."

"Can't it wait until tomorrow?" Trevor undid the vest's straps and slipped it up over his head. "Like she said, you've got security footage to confirm what happened, and I need to get her to the hospital."

Trevor handed the vest to Eric.

"Be at the station at nine." Eric took the protective gear and gave it an assessing glance. "Glad to see there aren't any new holes. I would've hated having to kick your ass."

Trevor chuckled. "You could've tried."

With a roll of his eyes, Eric turned to leave. "Derek and the rest of your team are waiting outside. Think the others are pissed they were late to the party." He stopped mid-stride. "Lex?"

"Yeah?"

His mouth curved upward. "Congratulations. You two are going to make great parents."

"Thanks, Eric." Lexi beamed.

The man's smile grew flat when he sent Trevor a final wave. "Nine o'clock sharp, Matthews. Don't keep my ass waiting."

Grinning, Trevor didn't bother to watch Eric disappear into the hallway. He was too busy staring at the mother of his unborn child. "Come on. Let's get you checked out so we can go home."

"It's just a couple of bruises. Really, I'm fine."

"You're pregnant, and you're going. End of discussion."

"Is that so?" She rose her brow playfully.

Trevor wasn't in the playing mood. That happened when you almost lost your whole world.

Linking his fingers with hers, he led her around the body and out the office door. "Humor me, angel. I'm barely hanging on by a thread as it is."

"Okay." Lexi leaned her head against his shoulder as they walked. "I'm sorry I worried you."

Ah, baby. He swallowed hard, his hand squeezing hers a little tighter. "Baby, worry doesn't even come close to describing how I felt."

He'd have nightmares about this night for months to come. Maybe forever.

The fear he'd felt knowing his wife's life—and their *child's* life—was in the hands of that son of a bitch....that shit still lingered inside him.

Trevor wondered if it would ever fully go away.

"Thank you." Lexi wrapped her free hand around his arm.

"For what?"

"For coming to save me. Again."

Trevor halted their movements and turned to her. Brushing a stray lock of hair from her forehead, he locked eyes with her and promised, "I'll come for you every time, angel. Every. Time. Don't ever doubt that."

EPILOGUE

LATER THAT NIGHT...

LEXI LAY ON HER BACK. LEGS SPREAD, HER EYES CLOSED. AND Trevor...Trevor played her body with perfection.

"Oh, God," she moaned, panting shamelessly as he thrust two fingers in and out of her greedy core.

His fingers strummed and plucked in the most magnificent ways. As if she were a priceless instrument, and he was the maestro.

"Like that?" he rasped.

Her head slid along the pillow in jerky nods. "Yes."

"You want more?"

"Please," she begged.

Even though, with Trevor, she knew she never really had to.

Always loving, always ready to give her what she *craved*, he put his head between her legs and swiped his tongue across her clit.

"Ah!" she cried out. Her body bowed, practically flying off the mattress.

Sensing her ravenous need, her intuitive husband picked up the pace. His fingers worked harder, faster, as he licked her clit over and over until she thought she'd die from pleasure.

And when her inner muscles began to quiver, he put the swollen bud between his lips and sent her flying.

Lexi came with an explosion of pleasure. Her climax so strong, so powerful, tiny stars actually flashed behind her tightly closed eyes.

Growling with pure, male satisfaction, Trevor slid his fingers from her body. She wanted to howl from the sudden loss, but then he placed his mouth over her weeping entrance.

When he finished drinking every drop of pleasure that he'd created, Lexi felt a trail of warm kisses moving up along her mid-section. Between her breasts. Just below her lips.

"God, you're beautiful when you come." He nibbled playfully.

"Pretty sure you just gave me the best Valentine's Day present ever," she teased.

"No, baby." Trevor got serious. "You did."

When the doctor found out she was pregnant, he'd ordered an ultrasound just as a precaution. Their baby was barely a spec, but they'd both fallen madly in love the second they saw their little miracle. And when they heard the precious heart-beat...they both cried tears of joy.

"Well, it's no *lasagna*."

His chest rumbled with laughter. "Pretty sure the stuff I tried to make wasn't either."

"It's the thought that counts."

That had been the second surprise Trevor had planned to give her. The first was the locket—which she was still wearing —and the second was a dinner made solely by him.

Since she was literally a chef, she usually did all of the cooking. It was sweet that he wanted to give her a break, but little did he know, she loved creating meals for him.

"To be fair"—Lexi smiled up at him— "it wasn't your fault you had to turn the oven off mid-bake and rush to my rescue."

"True." He gave her a quick kiss. "And I guess I can always try it again tomorrow."

"I say we focus on tonight." She moved her hips beneath his and urged him on.

Because watching her *husband* find pleasure was her most favorite thing to do in the whole world.

Moaning, Trevor closed his eyes and nodded. "Yes, ma'am."

Reaching between them, Lexi wrapped her fingers around his thick erection. Trevor hissed in a breath between his teeth, his cock flexing against her palm as she aligned the hot tip to her welcoming entrance.

He started to move, slowly working himself inside. She tilted her hips to give him better access, grabbed hold of his shoulders, and prepared for the glorious ride. And Trevor...

Stopped?

What the...

She stared up at him and frowned. "What's wrong?"

Concern flickered across his eyes. "You sure this won't hurt the baby?"

Lexi threw her head back and laughed. Oh, how she loved this overprotective man.

"Yes, honey." She cupped his chiseled jaw and smiled. "The doctor said sex is perfectly safe during the pregnancy."

His hot breath hit her chin just before he placed the softest of kisses on her lips. "Just wanted to be sure."

"I'm sure." She reached down, filling both of her hands with his well-defined rear. "Now start moving that hot ass of yours, Matthews."

One corner of his lips curved upward. "Getting saucy on me, angel?"

Lexi shrugged a shoulder. "Must be the hormones."

They both started to laugh, but then he finally *did* start moving his hot ass.

Filling her body to its limits, Trevor drew out every ounce of pleasure he could with each slow, torturous thrust.

In. Out. In. Out. In. Out.

Before long, their bedroom became filled with the sounds of their lovemaking. Heavy breathing. Skin moving against skin. Deep, satisfied moans laced with sin.

Except what they shared between them was anything *but* sinful.

It was beautiful.

Magical.

And it was all theirs.

It didn't take long for Lexi to fly over the edge once more. Trevor followed her shortly after.

Later, as she lay in the warmth and comfort of his arms, Lexi knew beyond a shadow of a doubt that nothing or no one would *ever* take away what belonged to them.

Because this man...this brave, wonderful man...he was her hero. Her *everything*. And together, they would always find a way to keep their family safe.

The End.

SEE HOW IT ALL STARTED WITH TREVOR AND THE REST OF R.I.S.C.'S ALPHA TEAM:

R.I.S.C. Series

Taking a Risk, Part One
Taking a Risk, Part Two
Beautiful Risk
Intentional Risk
Unpredictable Risk
Ultimate Risk
Targeted Risk
Savage Risk
Undeniable Risk
His Greatest Risk

ALSO BY ANNA BLAKELY

Charlie Team Series
Kellan
Asher
Greyson
Rhys

Bravo Team Series
Rescuing Gracelynn
Rescuing Katherine
Rescuing Gabriella
Rescuing Ellena
Rescuing Jenna

Marked Series
Marked For Death
Marked for Revenge
Marked for Deception
Marked for Obsession

TAC-OPS Series
Garrett's Destiny
Ethan's Destiny